FIELD TRIP FIASCO

By Kelli Hicks

Illustrated by Tatio Viana

Rourke
Educational Media
rourkeeducationalmedia.com

www.rourkeeducationalmedia.com

Edited by: Keli Sipperley
Cover layout by: Jennifer Thomas
Interior layout by: Rhea Magaro
Cover and Interior Illustrations by: Tatio Viana

Library of Congress PCN Data

Field Trip Fiasco / Kelli Hicks
(Rourke's Beginning Chapter Books)
ISBN (hard cover)(alk. paper) 978-1-63430-371-2
ISBN (soft cover) 978-1-63430-471-9
ISBN (e-Book) 978-1-63430-567-9
Library of Congress Control Number: 2015933728

Printed in the United States of America,
North Mankato, Minnesota

Dear Parents and Teachers:

Realistic fiction is ideal for readers transitioning from picture books to chapter books. In Rourke's Beginning Chapter Books, young readers will meet characters that are just like them. They will be drawn in by the familiar settings of school and home and the familiar themes of sports, friendship, feelings, and family. Young readers will relate to the characters as they experience the ups and downs of growing up. At this level, making connections with characters is key to developing reading comprehension.

Rourke's Beginning Chapter Books offer simple narratives organized into short chapters with some illustrations to support transitional readers. The short, simple sentences help readers build the needed stamina to conquer longer chapter books.

Whether young readers are reading the books independently or you are reading with them, engaging with them after they have read the book is still important. We've included several activities at the end of each book to make this both fun and educational.

By exposing young readers to beginning chapter books, you are setting them up to succeed in reading!

Enjoy,
Rourke Educational Media

Table of Contents

Chapter 1
Too Excited to Sleep

Barrett woke up earlier than usual. Darkness filled his bedroom. The only light he could see shone from the nightlight in the hallway. He yawned as he sat up and rubbed the sleep out of his eyes. The silence told him that the rest of the house was still asleep. Even his puppy was still snoring loudly from the end of the bed.

"Emma, today is the day!" His puppy stretched a little, grunted softly, and buried her nose under her front leg. Today was the day and he just couldn't wait any longer. Field trip day!

He climbed out of bed carefully, making sure he didn't wake the pile of legs still resting at the end of the bed. He decided to get dressed so he would be ready to go. He pulled on his tan pants with the big pockets, just in case he found any treasures on his trip. He tucked in his bright green school shirt with the purple lettering and tried to comb his hair. One little piece just wouldn't lie flat, but he hoped no one would notice.

Barrett's class would be traveling to a farm. He was so excited! He ate his French toast sticks carefully so he didn't drip sticky syrup on his shirt. Finally, his sister emerged from her bedroom and they headed off to school.

Chapter 2
Be My Buddy

All the kids rushed into the class that morning and put their backpacks away in the cubbies. Instead of putting his lunch in the cabinet, he put it in a big cooler filled with ice for the trip.

"Okay, kids," Mrs. Vee said, "everyone come sit on the floor and let's talk about the trip." The kids scrambled to the front of the room. They shushed each other so they could hear.

"Before we get on the bus, we need to talk about the rules. Everyone needs to stay safe and we don't want to lose anybody at the farm, do we?" Mrs. Vee smiled. "I'm not sure any of you are quite ready to be farmers."

The kids laughed. Some said, "Noooo!" Then they leaned in closer and tilted their heads so the teacher could see they were ready to listen.

"Rule number one," Mrs. Vee said, "please remember to stay with your buddy at all times." Their teacher started calling the names of the kids in pairs. Barrett crossed his fingers and looked around the room. Who would his partner be?

"Okay, Barrett, your partner is Nate. Be sure to stick together, boys."

Nate...Nate...YES! Nate was Barrett's best friend. They loved spending time together playing with Legos, being superheroes, and running around outside. He knew he had the best partner and together they would have the best time. As Mrs. Vee called the rest of the names, kids scooted next to their partners on the floor.

"Now that we have our buddies, here is rule number two. Make sure that you visit all the stations to enjoy all the activities. And third, have a great time! Now, let's line up and head out to the bus."

Chapter 3
Are We There Yet?

The kids marched to the bus, two by two, laughing and talking as they went.

"Hello kids, welcome aboard." The bus driver greeted the students with a smile and a wave and asked the kids to find their seats. "As soon as everyone is sitting down, we are ready to go."

The bus started with a rumble and a beep-beep, then pulled out of the parking lot onto the road. The kids were talking and someone starting singing. All the kids sang along, laughing and smiling all the way to the farm.

After a while, the bus pulled off the paved road and turned down a rocky dirt road. Dust flew up around the bus as it rumbled down the path. The bus grumbled to a stop, landing in a far corner of a grass parking lot.

"Yay! We're here! Yahoo!" the students cheered. They wiggled and bounced down the steps into the parking lot. A huge sign above the entrance read Old McMichael's Farm.

"Okay, everybody, find your partner and stick with the group," Mrs. Vee reminded them. The kids paired up and walked, bounced, or skipped through the gate.

Chapter 4
Which Way to Go

Barrett looked around. He couldn't decide what to focus on first. He could see tall brown and yellowish plants that looked almost like paper. That must be the corn maze, he thought. Tall stalks lined narrow walkways, creating a path that twisted and turned. Barrett thought it would be easy to get lost inside of it.

Barret was a little scared of the big maze, so he decided to wait and try that later. He saw games, a small store, a pumpkin patch, and animals––there was so much to see! The kids took off in different directions. Barrett decided to go to the pumpkin patch, but Nate started toward the corn maze.

"Nate," Barrett yelled, "we have to stay together." Barrett didn't want Nate to know he was a little scared, so he had a different idea. "Look how long that line is. Let's go explore the pumpkin patch instead."

Nate thought for a minute and said, "Okay, whatever."

The boys ran over to the pumpkins. Barrett saw some wooden picnic tables with scissors, markers, string, and papers shaped like pumpkins on them.

"Whoa," Nate said. "So cool!" Next to the table was a whole patch of pumpkins of all different shapes and sizes. Small, round pumpkins the size of soccer balls sat next to a huge, bright orange pumpkin covered with bumpy parts.

"Hey, that pumpkin is all warty," Nate said. "Ewww!" Many of the pumpkins were flat and a little brownish on one side from growing on the ground. It didn't seem to matter. There was the perfect pumpkin for every kid.

Chapter 5
Pumpkin Pie

Barrett found just the right pumpkin for himself. "This is it," he announced. "My perfect pumpkin." He picked it up carefully and began walking toward the tables. He looked up just in time to see that Nate found his perfect pumpkin too!

Just then, BAM! Barrett's friend Nico walked toward the table at exactly the same time and bumped right into him. Both pumpkins hit the hard ground with a splat.

Barrett and Nico looked at the orange mess on the ground. They looked at each other. They dropped their heads and tried to shake away the sadness.

"No problem boys, it happens all the time," said a young man wearing blue overalls and dark brown boots. "Do you know what happens now?" he asked. Both boys could feel the tears building. They just knew they were in trouble.

"No sir," they said at the same time.

"Well, what happens now is, I get to have pumpkin pie for dinner!" The man grinned a silly grin and both Nico and Barrett let out a sigh of relief, then a little giggle, then a big giggle. Soon they were both rolling on the ground laughing.

"Pumpkin pie!" Barrett said, relieved that he wasn't in trouble.

"Why don't each of you boys find a new pumpkin and I'll carry them to the table for you so that there aren't any more bumps or splats?" the man said.

At the table they found booklets from the teacher. She asked them to measure their pumpkins with string, count the lines around the pumpkin, and put it in water to see if it would float. Barrett wrote all about his pumpkin in the booklet and put it in the basket with the other finished books. Nico finished at the same, but couldn't find his partner.

"Oh no! Where is Eric?"

Barrett, Nate and Nico all looked for Eric. They looked under the table, around the pumpkins, and even behind the man in overalls. Just then, Eric jumped out from behind a tree. "Haha," he yelled, "I tricked you!" The boys sighed in relief, then fussed at Eric.

"Not funny, dude," Barrett said. "We thought you were lost!" Nate said. "Not cool, man," Nico said.

"Sorry guys, I was just playing a joke, it won't happen again," Eric said.

Chapter 6
Where Is That Kid?

Nico and Eric took off for the corn maze. "Hey," Nate said, "let's go to the corn maze too."

But Barrett wasn't ready.

"Wait," Barrett said. "What is that sound?" The boys listened carefully. It sounded like a little kid saying "Maaaa, maaaa." The boys tried to find where it was coming from.

It wasn't long before they did. But it wasn't the kind of kid they'd thought it was. It was a baby goat, which is also called a kid. They also discovered a lamb, a calf, a couple of rabbits, and a few chicks.

They'd found the baby animal nursery! The boys went through the gate into the nursery with the animals. The chicks pecked at the ground and peep peeped around the pen. Nate was pretty sure that one of the chicks was following him, trying to peck at his shoes.

"Hey chicken, that's my shoe, not your lunch," Nate said.

The lamb was small and puffy and white. It reminded Barrett of a big cotton ball. It looked like it would be soft, but it was actually rough against Barrett's hand. The calf stood swishing his tail back and forth to keep the flies away and moved his mouth so it looked like he was chewing. Every once in a while, he would let out a little moo and get back to chewing.

Barrett scrunched down and looked at the face of one of the bunnies. His little nose twitched back and forth, but he didn't make a sound. Barrett twitched his nose, just like the rabbit. It made Nate laugh. Soon Barrett, Nate, and their friends Aria and Kate were twitching their noses too. The girls seemed to like the bunnies the best of all the animals.

Suddenly, Kate yelled, "It's eating my shirt!" Everyone looked around and saw that the kid was trying to make a snack out of Kate's clothes. Aria got scared and ran out of the nursery. Now Kate was without a piece of her shirt and a buddy. Barrett and Nate took Kate by the hand and ran after Aria.

"Aria! Where are you?" The three friends looked around, but they didn't see Aria anywhere. In the distance a big, green tractor covered in dust rumbled and grumbled. A large, flat cart hooked to the back of the tractor was covered in hay. When the students looked closer, they spotted a head of brown, curly hair.

It must be Aria! The tractor grunted and puffed and looked like it was ready to start moving.

The kids ran as fast as they could to get to the tractor. "Hey, wait for us!"

The three of them ran as fast as they could. Their feet made pounding sounds on the pavement. They were running out of breath, but luck was on their side! The farmer driving the tractor looked up and saw the kids running. He stopped to wait.

"Welcome to the hay ride! Would you like to see what the rest of my farm looks like?" he asked the kids when they caught up to the tractor.

"Woo Hoo!" they all shouted and climbed up into the cart. Kate hugged Aria, she was so happy to see her.

Chapter 7
Scarecrows and Sneezes

The tractor grunted, then started to roll. They followed a long dirt path that circled around the edges of the farm. They saw rows of sprouts in the middle of brown fields and wondered what was growing beneath the green stems.

"I think those are pumpkin plants," Kate said.

"I think I see tomatoes," Aria said. They passed by a big, red wooden barn full of hay and stalls for the farmer's horses. Next to the barn, a family of pigs snorted and stomped in a muddy puddle. Barrett thought it would be fun to jump in the puddle with the pigs, but didn't think his mom or his teacher would think it was a good idea.

Achoo! Achoo! The hay made Barrett sneeze, but it was worth it to be able to enjoy this ride with his friends. Mrs. Vee told them to stay in pairs to be safe, but he wondered if she also knew the trip was extra fun with a buddy.

At the end of the hayride, the kids walked back toward the entrance of the farm. Nate felt like he swallowed a bucket of dust on the ride and the girls had yellow bits of straw in their hair and on their clothes.

"You look like scarecrows," Nate said laughing.

"We are scarecrows," the girls yelled as they stiffened their arms and legs and walked without bending at all. Barrett sniffled a little bit and sneezed a few times. The farm was alive with sound and movement: kids bustling from one area to the next, animals snorting, neighing, and mooing.

"Hey guys," Barrett said. "I need to blow my nose. Can we stop at the bathroom?" Barrett thought he saw the kids nod their heads.

He turned to the left and went into the bathroom. He blew his nose, and he blew it again. Then, washed his hands and his face and shook the extra water from his hands. He whistled a happy tune as he went out to join his friends.

"Hey Nate, want to trade sandwiches at lunch?" There was no answer. Barrett turned around in a circle, and found himself all alone. It wasn't just his friends who disappeared, it seemed everyone was gone. Barrett stood, trying to be calm, and trying to figure out what to do now.

Chapter 8
Who's Lost?

Barrett's forehead wrinkled and he tapped his toe on the ground. How could EVERYONE get lost on the farm? He thought for a moment, then scratched his head.

"I know," he said aloud. "Everyone must be eating lunch. I just have to find the picnic blankets." Barrett walked around the bathroom building. Nothing. Then, he walked past the little store. He noticed it earlier in the day. There was no one inside, just jars of homemade jam and little knickknacks and thing-a ma-bobs. He walked around one more time, just to be sure, but saw no one. He stood up on a bench to see if the blankets were in sight.

Again, nothing.

Barrett kept thinking, trying hard not to get scared. He walked back to where he and his friends took the hayride. The tractor was turned off, the dust settled, and the farmer had moved on to other chores.

The animal nursery was his next stop. He found the animals, some resting quietly now. A little peep, a small moo, a kid trying to eat his shoelaces, but no Aria, Nate, or Kate. "What am I going to do?" he said. Barrett walked toward the front gate. He found the picnic blankets, but no kids! "What is going on here?" he shouted. He was afraid to go to the parking lot to see if the bus was still there. What if it wasn't there? What if it was? Barrett looked for the games. Nothing. He tried to find the man in the blue overalls. He was nowhere.

Barrett sat on the ground with a thud. I like the farm, he thought to himself, but I don't want to be a farmer. What am I supposed to do? He put his head in his hands, then ran his fingers through his hair. He was afraid. It was the same feeling he felt when he thought about entering the corn maze. Oh NO! The corn maze! Maybe he should be scared, maybe everyone was stuck inside the corn maze and they needed his help. He didn't want to stay by himself with all of his friends and classmates lost. He knew he needed to be brave.

He stood up and brushed the hay and dirt off his pants. *Achoo!* He sneezed and wiped his nose on his sleeve. He pulled his shoulders back, lifted his head up high, and marched toward the maze. He wasn't going to let his fear keep him from saving his friends from the tall stalks. "I can do it," he said in a strong voice. "I can

do it," he said, this time a little softer. Can I do it? he asked himself. *Achoo!* "I can, I can, I can!" Barrett said bravely.

Barrett walked into the maze. It was shady and cool, the stalks towering over his head. He walked straight ahead until the path ended. He had to decide, right or left? "Turn left," said the voice in Barrett's head. "I can do it," he said aloud. Barrett followed the path. It wound around to the left, then back to the right.

"Is anybody there?" a voice called. Barrett thought at first he was talking to himself again, but realized it was a girl's voice.

"Aria, is that you?"

An excited voice responded, "It's me, it's me!" Barrett started running toward the voice and SMACK! He ran right into Aria. "Barrett, where were you? We couldn't find you anywhere so we decided to look for you in the maze and we all got lost."

"Remember, I said I needed to blow my nose? I went into the bathroom and when I came out everyone was gone."

"I'm sorry Barrett, I didn't hear you, none of us did."

"Okay," Barrett said. "Let's find everyone else, find our way out, and find some lunch! I'm starved!" Aria smiled and the two friends started walking. They curved around to the left, took another left, and followed the path to the right. Then they walked right into Kate and Nate. The kids jumped up and down happily, then kept walking to find their way out.

Around the next turn, they found Nico and Eric. A little later, they found Vincent and Chloe. Soon, the whole class was standing in a group right in the middle of the maze, still not sure how to find their way out.

"Kids, look up here!" It was Mrs. Vee. She stood on top of a platform that overlooked the maze. "Follow my directions and you will be out of there in no time at all."

Mrs. Vee talked the kids through the maze and they all piled out. "Anybody hungry?" she asked. The kids followed their teacher to the picnic blankets and sat down to eat.

"Barrett, do you want to trade sandwiches?" Nate asked. Barrett smiled and nodded at his friend. The students ate and talked about all of the day's adventures.

"Kids, it is time to get back on the bus. Be sure to bring your buddy," Mrs. Vee said. The students lined up two by two, then four by four, until everyone was hooked arm in arm skipping all the way back to the bus.

"No one is getting lost now! We are all sticking together!" Barrett said.

Reflection

My name is Barrett. My favorite thing in the world is to be with my friends. I try to help people and I try to be nice. I sometimes make mistakes, but I do what I can to make things better when that happens. I am afraid sometimes. I'm afraid of getting lost and afraid of being alone. I have bad allergies and I'm afraid that sometimes I won't be able to catch my breath or that I won't stop sneezing. Whenever I feel scared, I think about my friends and my family, and try to come up with a solution to make me feel better. I tell myself "I can, I can, I can!"

Discussion Questions

1. What did you learn about Barrett from the words the author used?

2. Why was it important for the author to use dialogue?

3. What was the problem in the story? How was it solved?

4. What effect did the setting have on the events of the story?

5. Is this book fiction or nonfiction? How do you know?

Vocabulary

Try using modeling clay to form these words. Talk about what each word means and use the words in a sentence as you shape them.

allergies
emerged
knickknacks
overalls
platform
scarecrow
stalks

Writing Prompt

Do you remember a time when you were afraid? Write about the situation you faced and how you decided what to do.

Q & A with Author Kelli Hicks

Have you ever been to a farm?
I have been to local farms a few times with students on a field trip and for birthday parties that my kids have been invited to attend. I really like visiting with the animals and I love going on hayrides, although they make me feel sleepy.

Do you have any allergies?
I am lucky that I don't have allergies. My son is allergic to many things, including hay and grass, which was the inspiration for the main character in this story. He gets really itchy and sneezy, but has learned to deal with it really well.

What are you afraid of?
When I was younger, I was not afraid of many things. I like spiders and snakes, and I don't mind the dark. However, now I am afraid of driving on a bridge over water. As a matter of fact, I'm a little afraid of swimming in lakes or oceans.

Connections

Do you want to help farmers in your community? Visit your local farms or talk with farmers about growing your own fruits or vegetables. When you can, buy produce directly from your local farmer.

Websites to Visit

Play farm games:
www.myamericanfarm.org

Farm facts, trivia, and activities:
www.farmsfoodfun.com

Learn about farm animals and the sounds they make:
www.kidsfarm.com

About the Author

Kelli Hicks is a teacher
and dog lover who lives
with her family in Tampa,
Florida. When she is not
teaching or writing, she
can usually be found
cleaning up whatever her
dog Emma June has decided to tear up.
She loves to be at the soccer field watching
her son and daughter play soccer.

About the Illustrator

My name is Tatio Viana. I was born, raised, and still live in Madrid. In order to do something "serious" while drawing, I studied advertising and actually worked as an advertising Art Director for many years, until in one of those famous mergers I was unemployed. So I dared to try what I love: illustrating. I have said "dare" because I am a self taught illustrator. I learned filling a lot of bins and enjoying the work of the thousands of illustrators I love.